To Adelle and Lucas,
may you always find the beautiful in the broken.
PETIT À PETIT, L'OISEAU FAIT SON NID.
—M.N.G.

For my mom and dad,
thank you for raising me with storytelling and picture books.
Thank you for being you.
—R.H.

Text copyright © 2019 by Melissa Nelson Greenberg
Illustrations copyright © 2019 by Ruth Hengeveld
Book design by Melissa Nelson Greenberg

Library of Congress Cataloging-in-Publication Data available.
ISBN: 978-1-944903-59-6

Printed in China.

10 9 8 7 6 5 4 3 2 1

Cameron Kids is an imprint of Cameron + Company

Cameron + Company
Petaluma, California 94952
www.cameronbooks.com

Oh, BEAR

STORY BY MELISSA NELSON GREENBERG

ART BY RUTH HENGEVELD

cameron kids

Bear got a kite for his birthday.

A bright yellow kite.

It was on a

long,

long string.

Bear was happy.

Holding tight to the string of the kite,

Bear began to run.

Bear ran through the meadow,

by the sea,

and back into the cool, hushed forest.

It was there that Bear's new kite got caught in a tree—

and ripped.

Oh, Bear.

Bird gently tugged at Bear's broken kite,
working hard to untangle it.

And when it was free,
Bird began to fly.

Bear felt a tug and looked up.

Holding tight to the string of the kite,
Bear began to run.

Bear no longer has a bright yellow kite, but Bear is happy.

He has something better.

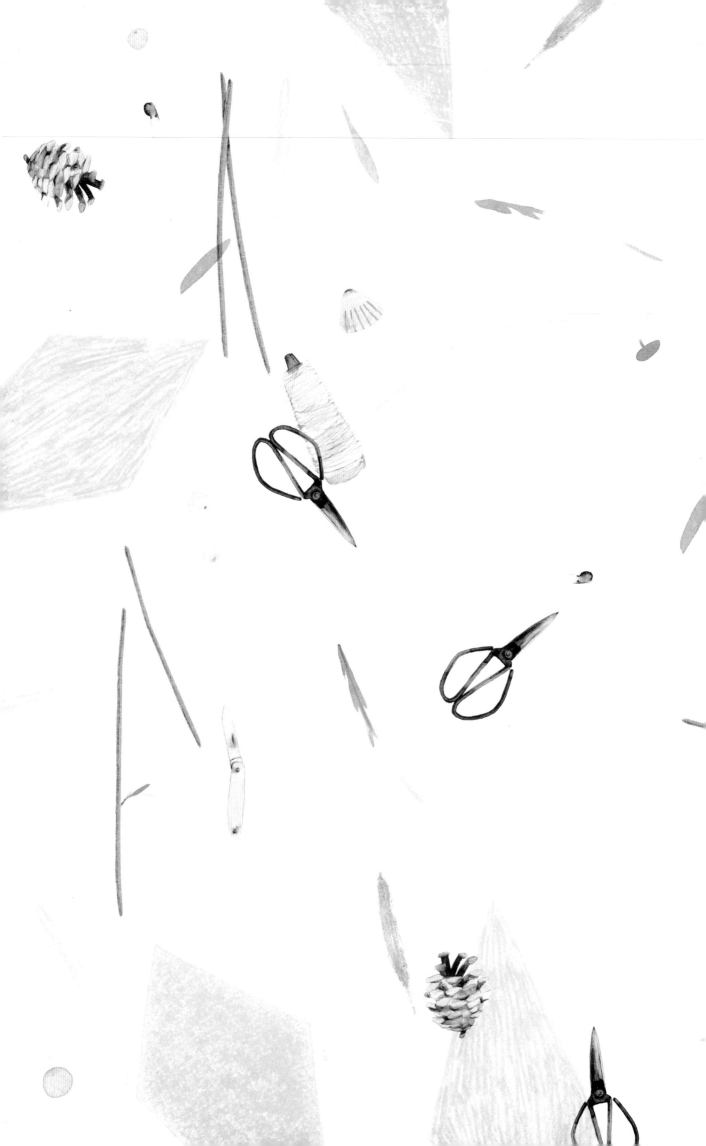